FOR OSCAR, PIPER, BO, AND SELAH
(WITH GRATITUDE FOR THEIR FATHER)
—N. D. W.

FOR MY DOG, ANN, WHO NINJA-SNEAKED
HER WAY INTO MY HEART
—J. J. H.

Text copyright © 2014 by N. D. Wilson
Cover art and interior illustrations copyright © 2014 by J. J. Harrison

Visit us on the Web! randomhouse.com/kids

Educators and librarians, for a variety of teaching tools,
visit us at RHTeachersLibrarians.com

Library of Congress Cataloging-in-Publication Data
Wilson, Nathan D.
Ninja boy goes to school. — First edition.
pages cm.
Summary: "A little boy explains what it's like to go to school—when you're a ninja." —Provided by publisher.
ISBN 978-0-375-86584-8 (trade) — ISBN 978-0-375-96584-5 (lib. bdg.) — ISBN 978-0-375-98179-1 (ebook)
[1. Ninja—Fiction. 2. Imagination—Fiction. 3. Schools—Fiction.] I. Harrison, J. J., illustrator. II. Title.
PZ7.W69744Ni 2014 [E]—dc23 2013033589

MANUFACTURED IN CHINA
10 9 8 7 6 5 4 3 2 1
First Edition

Book design by John Sazaklis

NINJA BOY GOES TO SCHOOL

ELEMENTARY

by N. D. Wilson

illustrated by J. J. Harrison

Random House 🏠 New York

It is hard being a ninja.

You must rise before the sun
and become one with the night.

You must possess the silence of a *GHOST*
(not the kind that wails and thumps) . . .

. . . the nimbleness of a MOUNTAIN GOAT
(but without the wool and horns) . . .

. . . the strength of a **GORILLA**
(but without the smell) . . .

. . . and the balance of a FLAMINGO
(but without looking silly).

It is hard being a ninja.
When you are a ninja, you will understand.

Ninjas must be one
with their surroundings.

A ninja must be still and patient,
like a deep-rooted tree . . .

. . . and strike with the *VIPER'S* speed when the time is right for disappearing.

A ninja's spirit is never caged.

Ninjas must never give up.

Even when facing a strong enemy.

A ninja knows when to be silent.

In the face of injustice and hardship, a ninja's emotions are as smooth and still as a clear pond.

It is hard being a ninja.

When you are a ninja,
you will understand.

Don't forget, a ninja must
learn to pretend that he is
not really a ninja . . .

even though he is.